FRIENDS
OF ACPL

THE CAT WHO THOUGHT HE WAS A TIGER

written and illustrated by POLLY CAMERON

Coward, McCann & Geoghegan, Inc. New York

Dedicated to Hank, Carolyn, Mike, Steve, Deborah, Marcia, Holly and Tory.

© 1956 by Coward-McCann, Inc.

All rights reserved. This book, or parts thereof, may not be reproduced in any form without permission in writing from the Publishers. Published simultaneously in the Dominion of Canada by Longmans, Green & Company, Toronto.

Tenth Impression

Library of Congress Catalog Card Number: 56-9946

MANUFACTURED IN THE UNITED STATES OF AMERICA

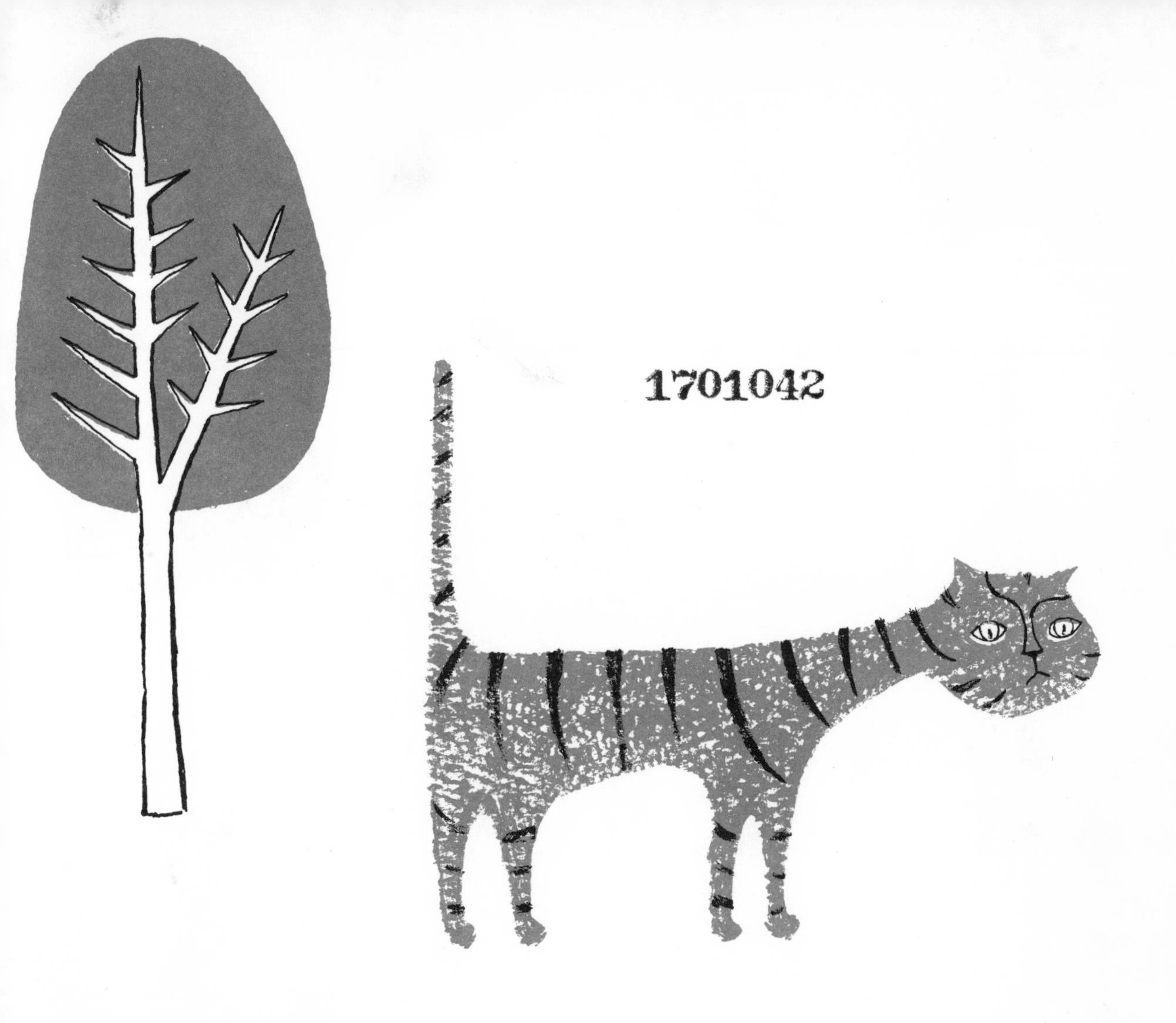
1701042

This is the story of the cat who thought he was a tiger.

His four brother and sister cats

and Hank and Carolyn

all lived together in a little house . . .

but he lived alone in the big back yard –
– because he thought that's what other tigers did.

They all ate together . . .

but he ate grass—because he thought
that's what other tigers did.

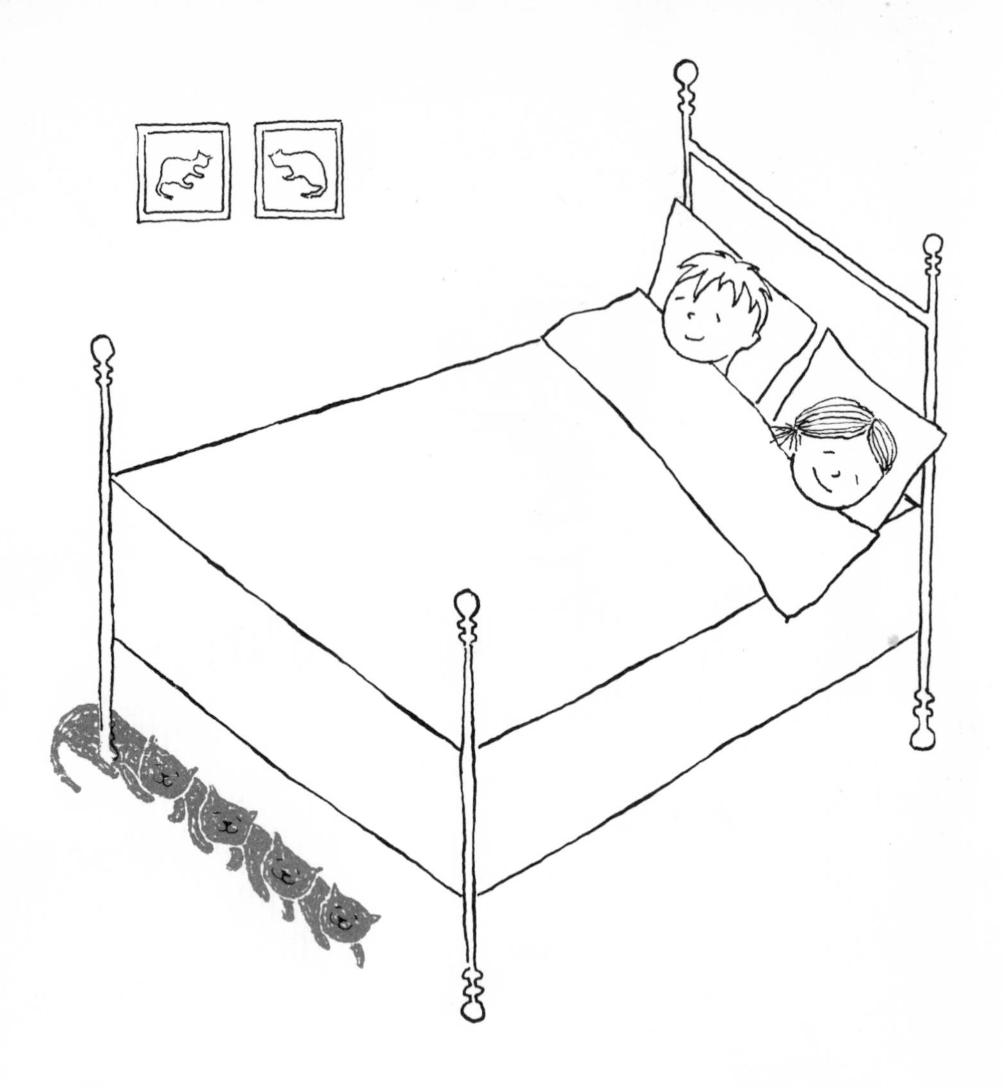

They all slept together . . .

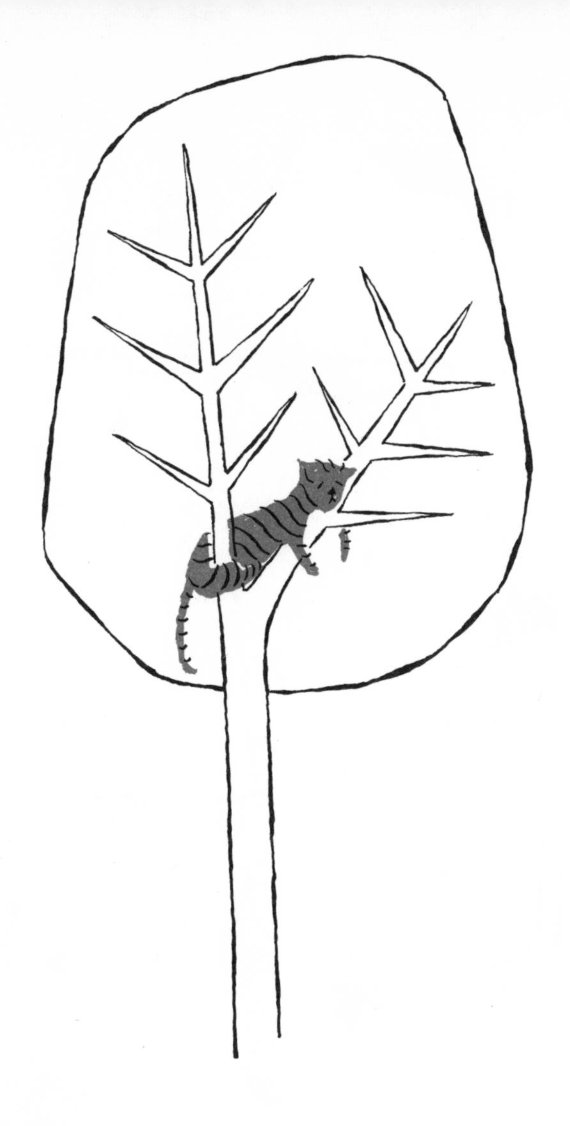

but he slept in a tree—because he thought
that's what other tigers did.

And they all played together . . .

but he played with his shadow –
because there were no other tigers in the big back yard.

Then – because he thought that's what other tigers did – he joined a circus.

He ate cotton candy – which made his whiskers sticky.

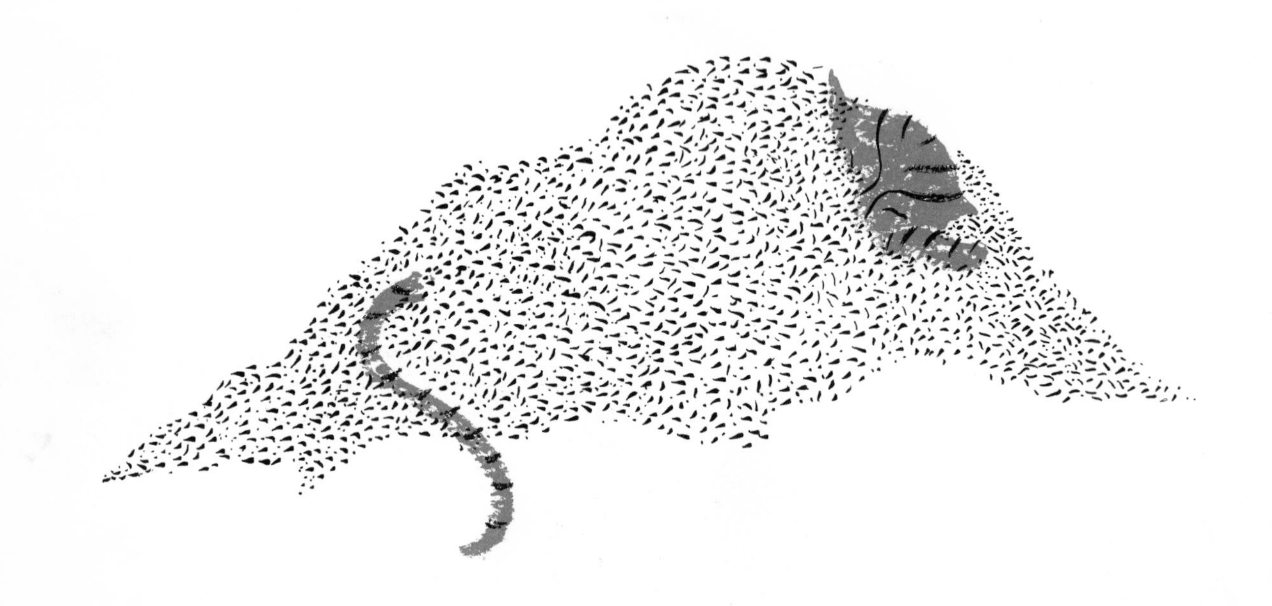

He slept in a pile of sawdust – which tickled his nose.

And he played with balloons – which always broke.

One day he wandered into the animal tent
and there he saw—

a TIGER!

“Hello there, Tiger,” he said. “May I play with you?”

"What? YOU play with ME?"
The tiger roared with laughter.

"Why can't I play with you?" asked the cat.
"You're a tiger and I'm a tiger."

"You? A TIGER? No you're not," said the tiger.
"You're a little cat."

"I AM?" he said.

“Yip-peee!” he shouted.

He left the circus and ran down the road.

1701042

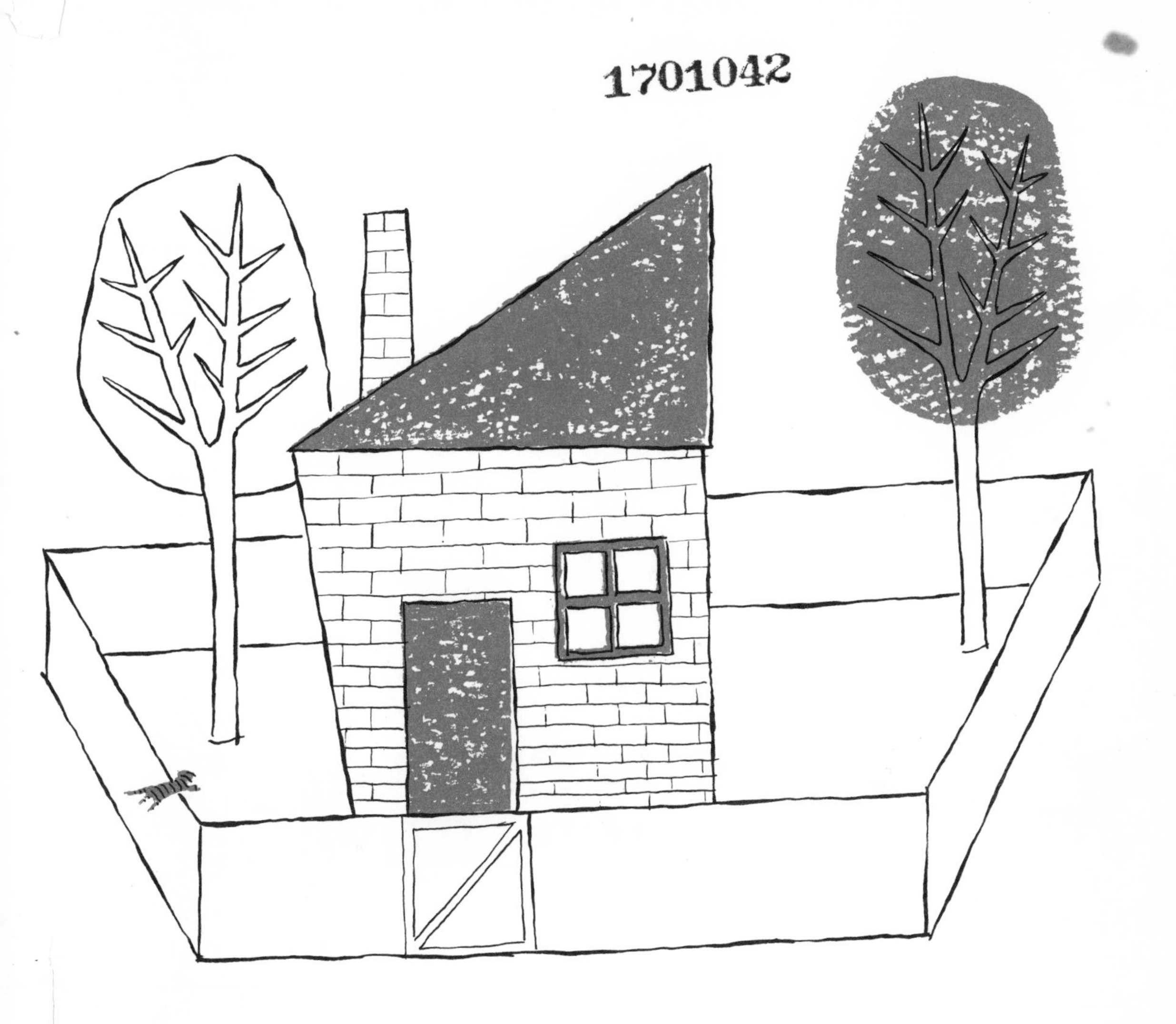

He jumped over the fence, through the big back yard and into the little house.

His four brother and sister cats and Hank and Carolyn all gathered around him. "I am a CAT," he said.

And everyone was simply delighted.

Now the cat who knows he's a cat
plays with his brothers and sisters . . .

and eats with his brothers and sisters . . .

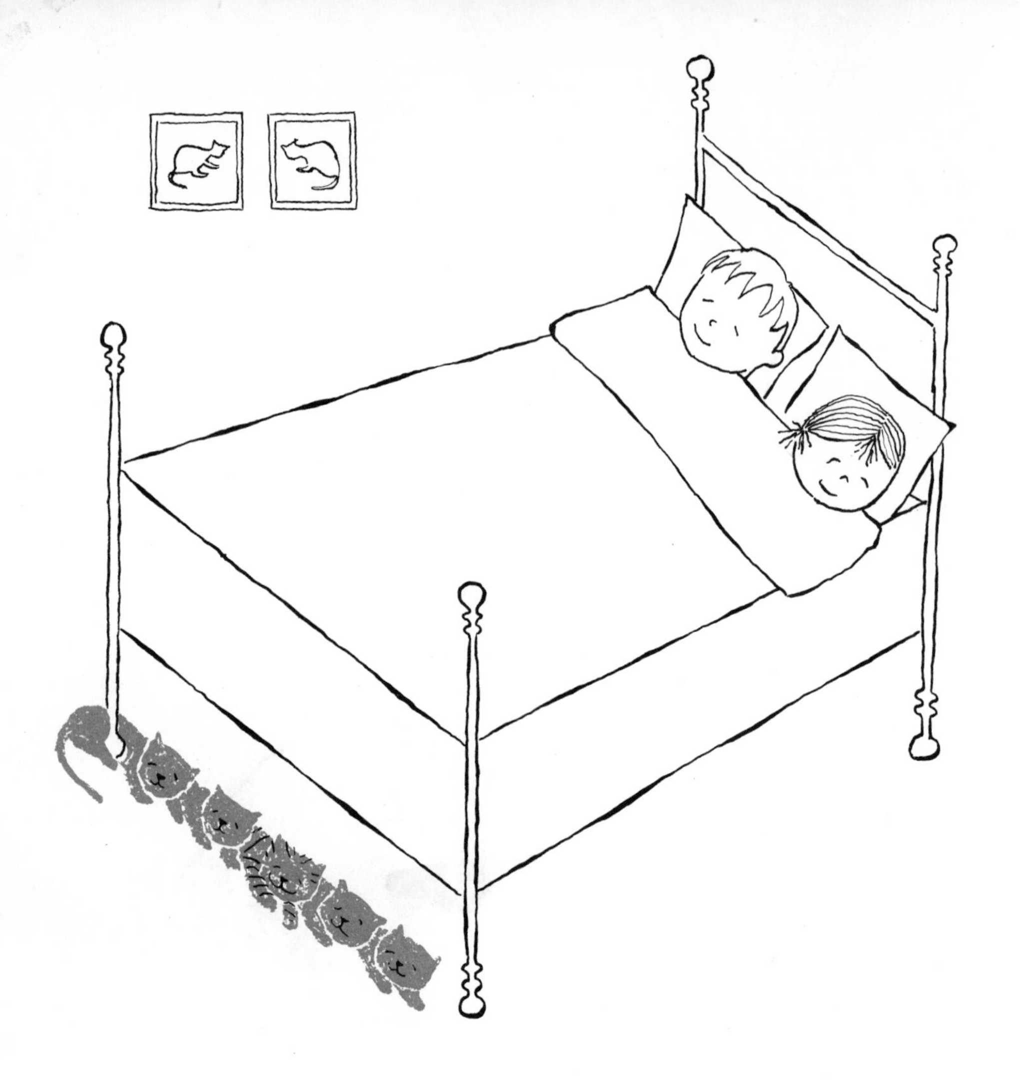

and sleeps with his brothers and sisters.

77 7009 15